Forbidden Entanglements

Shawn Davis

eBook ISBN: 978-1-966931-28-7
Paperback ISBN: 978-1-966931-29-4
Hardback ISBN: 978-1-966931-30-0

Dear Yolo Ent Supporters,

I want to take a moment to reassure you that your privacy is my top priority. I would never share any personal details or information about you. I value the confidentiality agreement we have with all our event attendees. The stories I share are about my own experiences and personal relationships.

As stated in our mission, YOLO ENT is a member-only organization that embraces the belief that we only have one life to live. We strive to create a safe and non-judgmental environment that welcomes individuals from all walks of life, regardless of race, gender, or sexual orientation.

This commitment to confidentiality and inclusivity is something I will always uphold.

Thank you for being a part of our community!

Table of Contents

Introduction

So here we are on a warm and boring night in Miami, Florida. Most of you would be thrilled to live in this crisp tropical climate next to the Caribbean, where lavish lifestyles are lived and thoroughly enjoyed. The nightlife is always alive, and people are out looking for adventure. But, for me and Ronnie, this was just another night to look for a bit of trouble, and let me tell you… Miami does *not* disappoint.

Let us back up and give you some context—earlier that evening, Ronnie and I were out having dinner and decided we were not ready to go back home; we wanted to party. As an avid *Lifestyle* member…yup, the upside-down pineapple crew is *Lifestyle*. This is the thing Us Swingers use to describe our culture.

A couple can be in the *Lifestyle* by attending events and becoming familiar with what goes on. They do not have to participate in the swapping and group sex that occurs there. Those that do participate are classified as "active."

I suggested a nearby swinger's party that was going on that night. Ronnie was not too keen on this idea due to her shy demeanor, but decided against her fears and said, "Fuck it!" Hold on…I am guessing you have some questions like, "Who are you?"

"Who is Ronnie, and why is she not a *Lifestyle* member?"

Or even "What exactly does *Lifestyle* mean?"

All fair questions – let's give you some more context: Ronnie is an educated, family-oriented, middle-aged Black mother who enjoys keeping things light and traveling the world…naked. Yup, she is a proud nudist who actively seeks new places where she can be her full self. In fact, she belongs to a community-based sorority. And, despite her freedom and active life, she longs for that special forever friend. Although she plays the innocent role, Ronnie can absolutely turn up and take on a wilder tone if the vibe is right.

I was a boy from the hood who turned choir boy to youth minster to being thrown out of the church altogether because of a free article being released about me being bisexual and knowing it at an early age. Despite this, I then returned to the church and became an ordained minister who became extremely successful…

But, unlike Ronnie, I do not believe in being subtle or shy. Although I also belong to a Black nudist group and a community-based fraternity, I prefer to be the group's troublemaker and extremist. What can I say? I don't lie, and I enjoy being myself despite what others may think of me. I guess I can see how that makes people uncomfortable sometimes.

Regardless, I am carefree and in my early 30's. I am a Black male, 6'3", 230 pounds and still behave like a grown child. Yes, I said a grown child. I am simply living my life without taking it too seriously, which is why I created (and embody) the model of living in the YOLO way—You Only Live Once.

Here's the kicker: before this, I was just a boy from the hood who became an extremely successful, well-respected, and influential leader in the financial industry, making a six-figure salary. You're probably thinking why I would leave such a prestigious position…that is a story for another time. And I digress.

Body – The Beginning

Now that you have a bit of background, back to that night. It all started with that boring night in the car, trying to figure out what to do other than going home and drinking like always. The silence between us felt heavy, both of us restless, needing something different. We both decided to go to this swinger's party in Miami.

For those of you who are not familiar with these types of house parties, getting on the invite list is quite challenging. But thanks to my connections, we were able to receive specific instructions, including a phone number to contact for the address—all in exchange for payment, of course. Yes, these parties are not only very exclusive but also beyond private. There's always a sense of stepping into another world, one where the usual rules don't apply.

Once we made the exchange and received the address, we were instructed to bring a bottle of our choice since it is BYOB (Bring Your Own Booze). And, because we were already on the road, Ronnie was worried about where we would stop to buy liquor since it was already late. To her surprise, though, I told her, "Don't worry. I always carry bottles for occasions like these." The look on her face was priceless; she hadn't expected me to be that prepared.

Although pitch black, we pulled up to this beautiful rancher-style house. The dim glow from the windows cast soft, mysterious shadows across the front lawn, making the house feel more like an invitation to a secret affair. Once at the door, the "greeter" (for lack of a better term) had us write our names on a clipboard. This was unusual to me as this was not an established *Lifestyle* Swingers club, but hey, we went with the flow and did as instructed. There's always a moment where you wonder what you're walking into, but that's part of the thrill, isn't it?

As we proceeded to walk through the house, we noticed most guests were bigger than normal. I could feel Ronnie's eyes widen as she scanned the room, realizing we'd just walked into a plus-size swinger's party. Truthfully, if I would've known, I would have never attended, as that is not my thing. But, as I mentioned earlier, I live by the YOLO mantra, so we decided to get a drink and relax. The vibe in the room was still charged, people mingling and whispering, the kind of atmosphere where you could either lean in or check out.

Some people were in lingerie, while others were fully dressed. Outside, they had some card games going on where you could smoke and hang out. The smell of cigars mixed with the night air gave the place an old-school, underground feel. They also had a table set up with sex games and prizes you could win. Deciding to make the best of it, we got ourselves some food and decided to see where this would take us. In the meantime, I decided to make the night a bit more interesting by inviting one of my guy friends, Magic, to the party. I needed something—or someone—to shake things up a bit.

Magic arrived at the party after midnight, which meant it was mandatory "dress down" time, meaning wear nothing but your underwear or less. Even in the dim light, Magic stood out like a spark—he had this energy about him that drew people in without him even trying. He resembled a modern-day, twenty-five-year-old Morris Chestnut.

So, naturally, of course, everyone's attention was immediately on him. It was like the air shifted as soon as he walked in, all eyes tracking him, a mix of curiosity and desire flickering across the faces in the room. Magic, on the other hand, was far from pleased with the guests as most, if not all, women there were obese. It was also an older crowd, and this party was his first "official" swinger's party. I could tell by the way he stood, arms crossed, his face tightening, that he was already over it.

Magic lost interest and decided to leave. He gave me a look before he walked out—one that said, "Next time, don't invite me to this kind of crowd." I guess it is all up to us now to have some fun…

Chapter 1 – Midnight

It's midnight now, and we are all dressed down in our lingerie and underwear. As usual, the sex games begin with the host, starting everyone off with introductions. To break the ice for any newcomers, she passed a microphone around the room, having people share something about themselves and what they are into. Of course, when it was Ronnie's turn to share, she said she was new to this whole "lifestyle" thing and had never been to a party before tonight. I immediately started to laugh because a statement like that automatically makes the men at the party go crazy. The room subtly shifted; eyes lingered longer, and the air buzzed with anticipation.

As expected, she immediately began to get lots of attention, and the side conversations broke out. I could see the curiosity and heat in the gazes around her. I made it a point to stick to her side as this all is new to her and can be a bit intimidating. One guy started a conversation with Ronnie and asked her some questions, one of which was if she liked her pussy eaten.

Ronnie was instantly put off and began to get bothered as it was forward and to the point. Her lips pressed into a tight line, and her eyes darted, searching for an escape. Seeing how uncomfortable she was getting, I answered for her and said yes but most men didn't know how to properly please her.

Taking it as a challenge, the guy invited Ronnie into one of the private bedrooms so he could show her that he knew how to eat pussy. To her surprise, the guy brought his friend to the room with him. Ronnie gave me a hesitant glance, and I nodded back—this was her decision.

As I stood on the wall watching Ronnie, the guy started to eat her out, and while Ronnie sucked his friend's dick. Her breath hitched at the first touch of his tongue, and I could see the tension melt from her body as she leaned into the moment. The guy who was receiving head from Ronnie looked over at me and waved to me to come over. I walked over, and immediately, of course, Ronnie pulled my dick out and began to suck it. There was something playful in her touch now, a confidence blooming as she played with us. She even started sword-playing with us, touching them together and playing with them.

The guy begins to get really turned on by this... in my head, I'm like, "Oh my god, why me? Not today!" I could feel the heat creeping up my neck, my control slipping bit by bit.

I really didn't want anyone to provoke me that night. This is a *straight* swinger's party… I cannot control myself, and I know it may make some people uncomfortable to see two men get at it… but here we go.

The guy begins to wrap his hands around my waist to give me support because one of my legs is bent to get close to Ronnie as she keeps trying to wrap her lips around both of our hard dicks. I wasn't expecting it at all, as he didn't seem like he would have those types of tendencies, especially one as intimate as grabbing onto another man's hips while he is naked—but I liked it, and I let it happen. He started rubbing my back up and down and getting really close to my ass. I could feel the little hairs standing up against my back. I could feel every touch, every shift, as if the air had thickened around us.

He no longer rubbed my back like a man; he instead began to caress my back more and more with softer, more intimate strokes significant of foreplay.

To my arousal, he slowly made his way down to my ass cheeks. My body reacted before I could even think—desire taking over reason. That's when I lost it and said, "Fuck it." Once the threshold was crossed, there was no going back. This is why I would rather not get involved once this shit starts, I don't know how to stop and I know exactly what to do. While no one was watching, I took his finger and slid it into my mouth and then guided it in between my ass cheeks. He obeyed, and at that point, I knew this guy wanted more than he was letting on to. His breath hitched, just like mine did earlier, and in that brief exchange, I knew we had crossed into new territory.

The night went on, and that steamy session came to an end. His name was TY, a "mans" man who had a thrilling erotic secret. Our bodies separated, but the heat lingered in the air, still thick with the echoes of what had just happened. The room had quieted, but a part of me stayed in that space, tangled in the heat of the moment.

Chapter 2 – TY

Before the party ended, TY and his friend invited another girl to play until they climaxed. Knowing they would probably leave soon, I told Ronnie to get TY's phone number. Her brow furrowed in confusion; she didn't understand why I was asking her to do that, but curiosity got the better of her, and she did as instructed. TY gave Ronnie his number right before they left the party.

We stayed for a while longer and played cards and watched the sex games between the other guests. As the night went on, we met a very interesting couple who had been married for 5 years with an age difference of 30 years. Their chemistry was palpable, a blend of playful banter and deep connection that intrigued us.

Although most others we met that night were ratcheted, it was amusing, and we had a great time. There was something about their dynamic that made us feel hopeful, a reminder that love could take many forms. Eventually, Ronnie and I were ready to call it a night. Little did she know I sent TY a text to see what he was up to with one thing in mind… round two. The anticipation buzzed in my veins, a thrilling reminder of the night's escapades.

TY replied, saying he was on his way home. I replied, telling him I was just about to drop Ronnie off and where home was. To my wonder, he said he was married (which meant I could not stop by his place) and that he was staying in West Palm Beach. I told him I lived in the same area, and he told me to let him know when I got close to my house so he could stop by to see me. A mix of excitement and nerves coursed through me, making me feel alive as

I rushed home to prepare—"cleaning out" meant giving myself an enema because I knew he wanted to fuck.

While I showered, the doorbell rang. The sound of the doorbell echoed in my chest, a thrilling reminder that this night was far from over. I jumped out and quickly dried myself off to go let him in. We walked upstairs to my bedroom, where TY wasted no time and began to passionately kiss me. Our tongues were in each other's throats as we held one another close and tight, as if this was what we were both longing for all along.

TY was a strong man, and he picked me up (yes, all 6ft 3' 230 pounds of me like nothing) as I wrapped my legs around him. I could feel his dick pulsing through his pants, a solid reminder of the raw desire simmering between us...

He threw me on the bed, and I immediately grabbed him by the waist. There was an urgency in my movements, an instinct to claim him as much as he claimed me. I gently pulled his thick dick out and started kissing the tip. I couldn't help but start to deep throating it, and his reaction was out of this world. He stopped me and said, "*I don't want to nut yet.*" His voice was firm yet teasing, and I felt a rush of adrenaline.

He put me on my back, pulled both legs up in the air, and began to kiss me again while softly caressing his thick dick against mine while teasing my ass with it. He kept shoving his tongue down my throat as he used his hands to put on his magnum-size condom... The sensation of his body pressing against mine was intoxicating, a blend of heat and anticipation.

Then, he slowed his pace and began to kiss me more deeply and softly as his thick head made its way into my ass. Suddenly, he picked me up off the bed and, out of nowhere, aggressively thrust his dick all the way into my ass.

I immediately screamed, *"Daddy, oh my god, what are you doing?!"* He completely ignored my cries and began to fuck me while holding me up in the air as if I was a straight bitch. In that moment, I felt both exhilarated and overwhelmed—manhandled in a way I never expected. I've never been manhandled like that so I felt like I really was his bitch in that moment. And, although I liked his aggressiveness, I had to stop. I told him *"TY, you can't fuck me like this!"* He said, *"okay then bust your nut."* He laid me down and I told him to get on his back because I wanted to bust all over his chest. The command felt exhilarating; it was my turn to take control, to revel in the pleasure. He excitedly pulled off the condom and began to stroke his throbbing dick up against mine. I felt such intense instant pleasure as I memorized over what was happening…

When we both started pulsating, I grabbed my dick and began to stroke it hard. I took his and began to grind it on my ass. There was a rhythm to it, a dance of bodies moving together, losing ourselves in the moment. I warned him not to put it in as I continued to stroke my dick harder and harder to a rhythm. I could tell he liked it because he got harder and harder and began to use one hand to choke me softly and the other to pinch my nipple. Just then, TY's throbbing dick penetrated my ass once again. This time, he grabbed onto my hips and forced me to ride it raw in an up-and-down motion. The sensation made me immediately bust, and I shot my nut all over him. Each pulse was electrifying, a release of everything that had built up within me.

As my tip kept squirting, his eyes shut, and I felt the pump deep in my ass. He was cumming. I felt the multiple shots of hot, warm

NUT. As soon as it was over, I annoyingly told him, *"Really, dude, did you really just do that?"* TY's reply was, *"Yeah… and I will be back tomorrow to give you more."* His casual confidence sent another shiver of thrill through me. The intense pleasure I felt was the beginning of an addiction.

Chapter 3 – Addiction

I slept like a baby that night. The next day came, and I noticed TY had texted me asking to talk on WhatsApp. December 10th, 2018 is where the first text messages begin to be exchanged between us. In the spirit of transparency, I have not altered the following dialogue:

TY – got you on here now

Me – kool, whats up

TY – Nothing much just getting to work, I am not allowed to have my phone inside work. But I come out and check my messages occasionally

Me – kool yea I no that part , hit me up when you want to come thru, even gym workouts are good

TY – lol cool definitely, yea I need those too, ttyl going in (end of initial conversation 12:36 pm)

TY – hey (start of new conversation 9:06 pm)

Me – whats up

TY – just got off

Me – kool, any plans tonight, how was work

TY – Nah she off but work was good

Me – kool, nice, when you wanna start the gym? Book your massage appointment? Etc. you could book a couple massage. I have another masseuse that can help with that.

TY – maybe we can start the gym next Monday

Me – kool

TY – I will try a single massage first and see how your work is. Lol

Me – fire, my work is just as good as yours

TY – well then I know it will be good

Me – I need a damn massage too

TY – I will try I am not the expert though

Me -you can massage something deep and ill be good

TY – hell yeah I can do that too. I take it did good

Me – yes sir fiending over here

TY – lol thanks I aim to please

Me – help me tonight, Christmas shopping

TY – I wish I could but I can't get out

Me – True

TY – Friday night Saturday night it's on

Me – word, both

TY – how many people coming to the card party

Me – not sure yet, waiting on a few confirmations

TY – I have a party to attend that is over at 9 then I will be over there

Me – I didn't know there's a swinger party in Miami Saturday so, what time Friday?

TY – I have a party Friday but I will be leaving there around 1 or 2

Me – 1 am?

TY – my other homie party is in Miami Saturday, are you going

Me – Nigga you and these parties

TY – I am popular what can I say, we can go to his party leave around 10 but if you do a card party it will end up as a swingers party?

Me – True

TY – I rather stay local because that drive is a killer

Me – I know but I could drive, how is party set up, you have the flyer

TY – (sends the flyer) I have a 80's 90's party so it will be late. So let me know about Saturday what you wanna do

Me – okay Ill have that figure out by Wednesday.

TY – so when the last time you was fucked for real?

Me- it's been a min, I'm thinking, probably a month ago, Whats up

TY – oh okay just was asking cause that ass was tight lol

Me – I wish I could more often, it's just hard finding real niggas down here in Florida.

TY – I feel you.

Me – My other homie ask could he watch since his girl out of town. Lmao

TY – he can join in too I like group shit

Me – I know that's whats up me too

TY – how long she gonna be gone?

Me – He probably will lol, she always be traveling

TY – tell him to come Friday night. Is he sexy?

Me – that's easy, we fucked chicks together, and caught head together from a drag queen he brought over 1 time.

TY – oh okay so he not into guys though

Me – he might bring this chick over we can ran a train on, he's into it somewhat

TY – okay cool, so set it up let me know I might slide out of the party even earlier lol.

Me – how often do you cum

TY – I cum a lot as I am stimulated and horny

Me – Damn I wish you could on me down tonight, let my boy watch

TY – damn would be nice, how would he watch via phone

Me – nope in person

TY – nice, I can't tonight wish I could. How about tomorrow night

Me – I will tell him, he probably will. It's going to suck cause I have gym 5am wed but

TY – it won't be long I get off around 10, I will hit you up later wife just got home.

Me- K

Chapter 4 – Best Friends

I went to bed that night thinking of that 6' 3" officer. Yup, this man who has been having these conversations and hidden physical encounters with me is a Police Officer in the county. At the time, I find it interesting. Especially since I felt that I had finally met a cool dude with a nice piece of dick close to home. All those thoughts made that night go so fast. The next morning, we hit the gym together as planned, just to do cardio. After that, we both showered, and he went off to work. Once again I started to get messages from TY: 10:33 am.

TY – (start of new conversation 9:06 pm) Good morning

Me – GM

TY – How is work

Me – ugh leaving work meeting now heading home, are you at work?

TY – no not yet in Broward not going to get an oil change

Me – Kool, that's far

TY – I had to go down there for something else this morning.

Me – kool, we good for tonight?

TY – Yes sir

Me – what time you heading to work, my homie bringing some chick over now lmao for a massage but I no she want more

TY – lol I have to be there by 1230

Me – lmao you late its 11:55

TY – Almost

Me - □ □ □

TY – omg just found out she, my wife took the night off

Me – OMG

TY – Yes she was supposed to work but had to use a day before the year ended or she would have lost it, going in I am late I will talk to you later

TY – (8 hours has passed since last message) I'm om way to you

Another hour passed before TY finally arrived up at the crib. At this point, I was just lying in bed but as soon as he arrived, I went to open the front door manually (I usually unlock it with my cellphone). Without hesitation, TY came in, took his clothes off, and got into bed with me. He immediately started touching me all over my body. He would grab my dick and stroke it because he knew it would get instantly hard when he touched me. It would drive me crazy the way he would stick his tongue down my throat, and when it was time for me to return the favor, he would suck my tongue as if it was a hard dick he was trying to take down his throat.

While he was kissing me, he lifted my legs up and rubbed some baby oil on the tip of his dick. At that point, I knew what was coming next… TY pushed his rock-hard shaft straight into me while holding me tightly. It felt so aggressive, and at the same time, he reached and stroked me to get me even harder. I began to call him daddy, which I obviously knew he would like and inevitably would make him fuck me even harder. I was to the point I would pretend I wasn't feeling it as much and hold my legs back to allow him to go deeper.

After he realized I was only doing that to bring the aggression out of him, he would tell me he wanted to see me cum, knowing he already came deep inside my ass. He would flip over on his back and tell me to sit across his chest, where I would stroke my dick as he grabbed my neck firmly and pushed his hard dick (yup, he would instantly get hard again even after he finished) between my ass cheeks while he pinched my nipples. That's my weakness, and of course, I squirted all over his chest. And although that was only about an hour, it felt more like five.

When we finished, he got in the shower because he knew his wife was home waiting for him, and the baby oil we used was too oily and noticeable on his skin. I knew that night was going to be another great well, rested evening for me, but he had other plans. He left, and I decided to relax a bit. I laid down to watch TV when, to my surprise, TY texted me telling me that if they didn't call him in for overtime, he would be back once his wife left and went to work. That text came in at 11:20 pm saying, "On my way in 10." He came back over and fucked me again for an hour. This time, though, he didn't leave—we fell asleep together with him holding me. At some point around 2:30 am, he got up and left.

Chapter 5 – Private Party

TY invited me to a local nightclub in West Palm Beach, where they were hosting a party that was 80s & 90s themed. This was not a swinger's party, though – it was a regular nightclub. The vibe sounded fun, full of nostalgia and energy, but I quickly reminded myself that this wasn't a swinger's party; it was just a regular nightclub.

After some texting back and forth, I told him it wasn't my scene and that I was not going to go. TY then told me that he was still going to go and would be drunk as fuck and that he probably was not going to stop by because *"drunk dick is a motherfucker, and you might be scared."* I laughed and went to bed, knowing he would probably get drunk and not bother texting me. His playful banter lingered in my mind, a reminder of our unique connection.

The next morning, I woke up to a bunch of missed calls and text messages. I replied, asking him what we were having for lunch. We spoke for a bit (small talk), and he told me he had been spending time with the family but nothing interesting. His words felt comforting, like the ease of a familiar friendship that had grown deeper over time.

At this point, I was really digging this friendship… It was like I had the best of both worlds: a best friend I loved hanging out with and a person I could play with and be myself. In fact, pretty much every other day, he would bring me lunch, and we would eat together. It became a ritual that I cherished, a blend of companionship and camaraderie. On top of that, we regularly started working out together with my personal trainer twice per week, which I introduced him to. My favorite part, though, was the steamy showers after the workouts… I can imagine that at this point you know why.

We developed a daily routine of meeting up at night and having fun. The anticipation of seeing him became a highlight of my day. I could tell that I was really starting to trust TY because I allowed him to use a sway bar on me. It was a significant moment, a step into deeper intimacy and vulnerability. The sway bar that you use to tie your two hands to your feet together. It's impossible for you to move once you are tied. Whether you are on your back or on your hands and knees, it's impossible to move as you are at the mercy of the person who tied you. Although an intense experience, it was fun.

One night, he texted me what was up, so I told him that I would show him how I like to be treated, using a bitch, as an example. Intrigued, he said which bitch, and I told him there were two girls coming. One of which was a girlfriend that wanted to get gangbanged. His interest piqued, and I could feel the thrill of our playful exchanges taking a daring turn. He told me he was interested and to call him. The couple arrived at my place.

The male was in his thirties, and the female was in her 40s. We started off with drinking, playing games, and just feeling each other out. The atmosphere was charged with excitement, a dance of flirtation and anticipation. When she got comfortable, TY and I took the woman to the bedroom, where we immediately got our dicks sucked and took turns fucking her as her husband watched.

In the middle of it, we did double vaginal penetration (or DVP, for short), which was a first for her, but she loved it. What got my attention, though, was that I caught her husband looking at me while we were DVP'ing his wife…

There was an unspoken understanding in that glance, a shared acknowledgment of desires. At that point, I *knew* that he was into the same thing. Things like these are common; most people are afraid to express what they truly like, so I didn't make a big deal out of it.

As we DVP'ed, the intensity heightened because both our dicks were rubbing against each other, amplifying the sensation of sex. The pleasure was electric, a visceral connection that transcended our individual experiences. Once we both came, the wife thanked us and told us she had a great time as it was the first time she had ever done anything like that. She even said, *"You know, for me to be a 62-year-old, how do you think I did?"* TY and I looked at each other in complete amazement; that had to be the oldest woman we've ever fucked! But you know what they say… black don't crack. Her vibrant energy was infectious, and I admired her daring spirit.

After that experience, we would continue to hang out regularly. We would go to the gym together and work at our jobs, and whenever I was working locally, he would find me throughout the day to bring me lunch, say hi, and give me a kiss. It became our little ritual, a sweet reminder of our bond amidst our busy lives. We had established a routine and got used to seeing each other all the time. But I decided to go on a nudist cruise, which meant it would be the first time TY and I would not see each other. The thought of being away from him left a hollow feeling in my chest, a testament to how much our connection had grown. I invited him to join me, and he said he was really interested and said he would go.

The only problem was how he was going to tell his wife he was taking a trip with me. His wife said no, and she wouldn't let him join me or come with us on that trip. The reality of his married life loomed over us, a constant reminder of the boundaries we navigated. I went without them and every day I was there, we would always talk through text messages, and he would even sing me songs. Songs like "My First Love" echoed through my mind, and I couldn't help but laugh, feeling a mix of affection and longing.

Chapter 6 – Date Night

When I came back, we didn't miss a beat. We continued to hang out together, but eventually, I brought up the fact that his wife was always asking him where he was every time he would come to my area. We both found it strange, but I told him it IS what it IS and did not pay to much attention to it. I even told him, *"Why don't you just bring your wife?"*

TY told me he just couldn't tell her that. At one point, after TY had stopped by his place to drop some stuff off, he told me that his wife's iPad kept pinging over and over again. He looked at it, and it said "Geo-Location."

I Googled it and immediately told him, *"Yo, your wife got a tracker on your car."* I took a picture of it and sent it to him. I told him to look for the device in his car, and sure enough, he found it underneath his car. He was livid and really upset. I tried to calm him down and recommended him to just come clean and tell her and even invite her to be part of the *Lifestyle*.

Eventually, he broke down and decided to tell his wife the truth. He told her that I was his homeboy who had sex parties and gangbangs in the house. He told her that he was just a voyeur—someone who just watches and does not participate—in these events. To my surprise, his wife told him that she wanted to see it for herself. I thought it would be a great idea, so I went ahead and scheduled a gangbang for one of my regular clients, who was always down to fulfill her fantasies.

That day, the guests arrived, and along with TY and his wife, we embarked on an unforgettable journey into the unknown. They watched the entire time, absorbing the experience, but afterward, TY's wife turned to him and asked, "This is what you're into? This is what you look at?" Her disbelief was palpable, likely stemming from the fact that the woman getting gangbanged was nowhere near as beautiful as she was. She found it odd that he enjoyed that. What she didn't understand is that this Lifestyle is not about appearance; rather, it's about fulfilling fantasies without judgment from others.

Since TY's wife was clearly not happy, I recommended we go to Trapeze in Fort Lauderdale because I knew I was not hosting any events for a while and this way, she would be able to get what she wanted to see plus witness the environment TY was actually into. She was down and we decided to make it a double date. Of course, I naturally chose the baddest girl I know, who was badder than Queen B herself, to come with me to Trapeze and be my date.

That night, we brought bottles of liquor to the club. The atmosphere was electric as we danced and drank, excitement building as we took TY and his wife on a tour of the club. But before we could head to the back, it was mandatory to stop by the locker room to change before entering that area. Men must be in towels, while women can wear lingerie.

Everyone got undressed, the women slipping into their delicate lingerie while TY and I wrapped ourselves in towels. Together, we walked to the back of the club, where I took the time to explain the different areas, the rooms, and the etiquette of swinging. I prepared TY's wife for what to expect, explaining how to navigate the social dynamics and what to say or not say in various situations.

As we continued hanging out, walking around and drinking, we soon found ourselves in the main couch area. TY and I sat down, delving into deep conversation while our dates lingered nearby. Suddenly, my date leaned over and started giving TY's wife head. What began as casual conversation quickly turned into an unexpected spectacle, as my date devoted herself to TY's wife for three straight hours. We didn't even realize how much time had passed, completely lost in our discussion while ensuring that they remained undisturbed.

When TY's wife finally came out of the trans she was in, she got up and said, "oh my god, does this mean I am bisexual? Does this mean I am a lesbian?" I started laughing, and TY told her, "babe, you know, don't say that; don't feel that way. Because you know how you just got head for 3 hours and it was good? That is kind of what he (me) has been doing to me…" Surprised, she said, "for real?! Oh, I want to see!"

Surprised, she raised an eyebrow. "For real?! Oh, I want to see!"

We left the club buzzing with excitement, and I dropped off my date back at her place. TY and his wife wanted to come back to my house, and the thrill of the night was only just beginning. We took shots together, laughter filling the air as we transitioned from the club to my home. The atmosphere was charged with anticipation, leading us to an unforgettable experience: a threesome.

As we explored each other's bodies, I couldn't help but marvel at the taste of TY's wife. Her pussy tasted like nothing I had ever encountered before—sweet and intoxicating. It wasn't about the scent; it was the flavor that drove me wild. As TY and I continued to pleasure her together, we found ourselves kissing and licking, our tongues entwining in an electrifying dance while still pleasuring her.

I could feel the heat rising, the intensity growing, and I knew he was ready to move on. Leaning closer, I whispered into his ear, "You want me to put this dick in your wife?" His affirmation was swift, but he had a playful request: he wanted her to sit on his face while I fucked her. I loved the idea, the thrill of it igniting something primal within me.

As we began to fuck her, TY took turns licking her pussy and sucking my balls. Each stroke back and forth felt electric, the wetness building with every moment as he made her squirm. Our synchronized movements created a rhythm that left us breathless, and as I withdrew to catch my breath, he slid my dick into his mouth, and I found myself thrusting back into her.

That experience brought us all closer together. What began as a secret grew into a bond forged in shared desires and exploration. I invited them to my parties, and she soon became my door girl, a vibrant presence in the space I had created. We crafted a Lifestyle name for her so she could introduce herself to others seamlessly.

Over time, she became familiar and comfortable in that realm of parties, her laughter echoing through the nights. She would often crack jokes, her sense of humor shining bright against the backdrop of wild stories and even wilder encounters. Sometimes, she would even see her coworkers attend the parties, their presence weaving new relationships and friendships, bridging the gaps between their everyday lives and the thrilling escapades we all shared.

Chapter 7 – ATL

Throughout this newfound relationship, we were pretty much-having threesomes all the time. My birthday was coming up, so I decided to invite them both to Atlanta to celebrate. I bought them plane tickets and flew everyone else up to Atlanta. I rented an Airbnb in downtown Atlantic Station, where everyone crashed into different rooms throughout the rental. Each night (all five nights), we kicked off the parties by hitting Trapeze. The vibe changed every night—sometimes wild, sometimes chill—but one thing stayed the same: TY's wife always wanted it to be all about her. The way she acted, it was like it wasn't even my birthday anymore.

One night at Trap (short for Trapeze), she straight-up refused to do anything I wanted to do; it had to be her way or nothing at all. So, I backed off and let her do her thing, trying to respect their dynamic. But it rubbed me the wrong way. I figured once they were done doing whatever they wanted, then I could go off and enjoy myself. That night, I played it cool, let them have their fun, and when it was over, I drove them back to the Airbnb in Atlantic Station. Everyone got out of the truck and headed inside, except for TY. He lingered, looking at me all confused. "Wait…where are you going?"

I shouted back, "I'm going out to enjoy my birthday. It's my birthday weekend, remember?"

TY's face tightened. "What? You're just going to go out by yourself? You've been drinking. You can't just drive around and go out. You need to come upstairs with us."

I responded; "I couldn't believe it. Bro, I'm grown. I'm going to go have fun. Y'all had your little night doing whatever you wanted. I didn't get to do shit I wanted to do…so bye." Meanwhile, his wife was just watching, giving him that look like, "Why are you acting like this with him? Let him go. I'm here; you're supposed to be up there with me. Why are you sitting here arguing with him?" I told him he better go upstairs with his wife, and he finally went in. I hit the streets, driving around to all the hotspots I knew.

As I drove around, my phone kept blowing up with calls and texts. I ignored them at first, but when I looked closer, it was TY. Something felt off. Why was he so damn fixated on me? I hit up three different spots in Atlanta—two were shut down, and the other one was dead. I wasn't about to waste money on some lame spot, so I decided to head back to the Airbnb in Atlantic Station.

When I got back, I parked on the street, and there it was again—TY calling me non-stop. I finally picked up, and he was all up in my ear asking why I was out, why I wasn't upstairs with them. I told him I was just chilling down stairs in the car, but he insisted he was coming downstairs to see me. I asked him to bring me a drink, and he came out to the car, hopping in like he was my man or something.

The whole time, I'm thinking, "This dude really left his wife, who's probably up there pissed, to come sit with me in the middle of the night?" We sat in the car, and TY was acting like a jealous boyfriend, whining and going on. I had to set him straight. "Dude, we're not in a relationship! Your wife is upstairs." But in TY's mind, he was clearly feeling something else.

That's when it hit me—TY was catching serious feelings. I felt that shit, too, sometimes, but every time it crept up, I'd shut it down.

This wasn't supposed to be that. TY kept begging and pleading for me to go back upstairs with him. By now, I was definitely tipsy from the drinks.

I said screw it and went back upstairs to the loft, where TY's wife was lying in bed. She turned over and asked, "You good?"

"Yeah, I'm fine, but y'all aren't. Y'all need to go get counseling," I shouted back. I laid down, turned my back to them, and passed out.

The next morning, TY's wife came up to me, looking serious. "Do you know what you said to me last night?" I nodded and told her I remembered saying that y'all needed counseling. She looked taken back. "What? Why would you say that?"

"Because this Lifestyle is new to you, and y'all don't get it yet. I think it'd be better if a counselor explained it instead of me." She nodded, a little lost, but dropped it. For the rest of the trip, I made a point to keep my distance from them, focusing on doing me.

When we got back home, they said they wanted to come over to my place to talk. I told them to come through, and I cooked up dinner—a homemade pot pie, salmon stuffed with crab meat, and some greens. I love whipping up everything from scratch; the whole process calms me down and lets me zone out. We ate, laughed, and killed two bottles of wine together.

TY's wife got serious and asked, "What is this? What are we in?" I broke it down for her—this situation was pure swinging for me, but some people might call it poly.

I explained, "Polyamorous means being in an exclusive relationship with multiple people, whether it's same-sex or opposite-sex, but everyone's tied together in some way."

She took a deep breath and asked if that was what we had going on. I told her, "If you're sure this is what you want if you can handle it, then I'm down to try it." She paused, then said, "Well, I don't want you having sex with other people while also having sex with us."

I shrugged. "Alright, cool. I'm down with that."

The vibe shifted. This wasn't just some casual thing any more. This conversation flipped everything on its head. It was messy, uncharted territory we were stepping into, but something about it felt right like this was where we were supposed to go next.

Chapter 8 – Our Wife

Truth be told, I had everything I needed, and that's why I agreed to be in this polyamorous relationship with them. I had the man, and I had the woman—everything was good. In the beginning, it felt like a dream. We shared laughter, late-night talks, and the kind of intimacy I had never known. For a while, our new relationship worked. We navigated this uncharted territory together, reveling in the thrill of exploration and the bond we forged. But, eventually, I found out that TY was still out there fucking everybody else while she did the same, meeting up with other couples.

At this point, I thought to myself, "Wait, me? I'm the only one that's not doing anything? Ohhh nooo…" I called it off and told them that we couldn't do this anymore. The realization hit me hard: I was the only one remaining loyal in a relationship that was supposed to be about mutual freedom and respect. It was a bitter pill to swallow, knowing I was giving my all while they were living their best lives without me.

We continued going to parties together anyway. One time, after everyone else had already left, we were playing around, and of course, TY and I made her cum, then TY, but I never did. The atmosphere was charged with excitement, and I felt a strange mixture of jealousy and curiosity as I watched them. It was exhilarating and frustrating all at once. She then called me by my name and said, "Hey, I want you to cum too… how do you want to cum?" I laughed and chuckled, and she again asked me the same question.

I said okay and told her to sit on TY's face, so she did. I sat across TY's waist, and of course, the meat went right to my ass. As I positioned myself, I felt a rush of adrenaline mixed with vulnerability. It was as if I was stepping into a new role, one that blurred the lines of our relationship even further. I told her to suck on my nipples. As we did that, having multiple senses being stimulated at the same time made me cum. The release was intense and unexpected, and I could see the shock in her eyes—it felt like a new connection was forged in that moment.

After that, things were cool for a while. We would go out together all over Florida to restaurants, lounges, nightclubs, and even to the casinos. Every outing felt like an adventure, each place we visited leaving a mark on my memory. I cherished the freedom we had, yet I felt a nagging concern in the back of my mind. Those experiences were really eye-opening and interesting to me. For the remainder of the time, they became my permanent staff at my events.

At one particular event, as it was dying down, TY's wife was tired, so I told her to go lay down in my room after I had cleaned up and changed the sheets. As I lay beside her, I couldn't help but feel a mix of affection and apprehension. She looked at me and asked, "Oh, where's TY?" I got up and went downstairs to find him. There were only about 3-4 people left (mostly my staff), and I saw TY right there standing up, getting head from a dude. The sight was jarring—an unsettling reminder of the boundaries we had blurred.

I thought to myself, "Oh god… boy…" I approached him and said, "Yo, yo wife is upstairs looking for you, and you down here getting head." I made him go back upstairs, and we just chilled. But the moment lingered in my mind, a heavy weight that I couldn't shake off. It felt like we were teetering on the edge of something dangerous, and I wasn't sure how long I could balance on that ledge.

The next day, it came to me: wait… you're playing a dangerous game because he's having sex, and we are not protecting ourselves. The only thoughts that were going through my mind were that his wife only knew it was me—she didn't know he was out there being promiscuous and doing other people. To protect myself in case something happened, I knew I needed to break off the relationship altogether or at least the sex part.

Chapter 9 – The Breakup

I invited TY over in the morning before work. He arrived in his uniform and sat right on my steps. His presence felt heavy, like a storm cloud looming over us, and I could sense the tension in the air. I told him it was over. He begged me not to leave the relationship that we had. There was a desperation in his voice that tugged at my heart, but I knew I had to stay firm, even as my resolve wavered. I explained the reasons for it and told him I couldn't do it anymore. I was strong in my tone and felt fine during the entire thing, but from the looks he was giving me, I could tell he was angry, confused, and disappointed.

After I finished, he said, "Okay, well, if that's what you want, then that's what it is," and he left. Those words echoed in my mind, but as the door closed behind him, the weight of the moment crashed down on me.

The moment he left, I started crying and screaming. The tears flowed freely, a torrent of emotions I had been holding back. Each sob felt like a release, but it was also a reminder of everything I was losing. I felt like everything had just crashed. This was the point where I knew I was actually in love with him. The realization was both freeing and suffocating—love was supposed to lift you up, yet here I was, crushed beneath its weight. It hurt so bad to call off the relationship.

I sat there for what felt like hours, my heart aching as I replayed every moment we shared, from the laughter to the intimacy. I later found out he had fabricated a story to tell his wife. The betrayal cut deeper than I had anticipated, leaving a bitter taste in my mouth. TY told her that the reason I had broken off the relationship was because I tried to take him away from her. His words twisted the truth into something ugly, and I felt my heart sink as I imagined her hearing that, picturing her pain and anger.

I know he did this because he was hurt just like me. Hurt people… hurt people, so he, of course, tried to hurt and discredit me. It was a defense mechanism, a way to shield himself from the fallout, but it felt like a dagger aimed right at my heart. The thought of being painted as the villain in our story was unbearable.

In that moment of anguish, I questioned everything—our connection, his feelings, and my own worth. Did he ever truly care for me, or was I just a fleeting escape from the reality he didn't want to face? My mind raced with memories, some sweet, others laced with doubt. I remembered the laughter we shared, the dreams we painted together, and the quiet moments when everything felt perfect. But now, they felt tainted, overshadowed by betrayal.

As I sat there in the aftermath, I couldn't shake the feeling of being discarded, like a chapter he was ready to close without a second thought. The tangled web of emotions left me feeling lost and vulnerable, questioning everything about our time together. It was a harsh lesson in love's complexities: the thrill of passion can quickly turn into a deep sense of loss, leaving scars that take time to heal. I realized that love, in all its forms, could be both a blessing and a curse, capable of building us up and tearing us apart.

In the days that followed, I struggled to find my footing. I tried to move on, but the weight of the memories clung to me like a shadow. I felt trapped in a cycle of grief and anger, questioning what I truly wanted from love.

Chapter 10 – Star

Three Months Later

During one of my biweekly party events, I noticed a new girl who immediately caught my attention. She was this stunning 5'6" – 5'7", 140ish-pound, caramel-colored woman who came to the party in the company of a guy I knew who was a regular at my events. Her presence radiated confidence, and her smile was infectious, drawing people in. I knew they were just friends, though—I knew the guy she was with was married. Because I was working, and I pride myself on being professional during my events, I didn't engage her and did not really approach her during the event unless it was as the party host. I could feel the curiosity bubbling within me, but I reminded myself that professionalism was key. When the time was right, though, and I had a moment to break off, I did ask her for her number so I could talk to her later on after the party. Her name was Star.

After about a week of talking, we spent a few hours getting to know one another over the phone. Our conversations flowed easily, filled with laughter and shared stories. We learned about each other's backgrounds—where we were from (Star is originally from North Carolina, and I am from Baltimore)—and just spent some time getting to know one another in a friendly way.

During Thanksgiving week, Star did not go home for the holidays, and neither did I, so she invited me over for a small Thanksgiving get-together with her daughter. The warmth of her home enveloped me as soon as I walked in, a stark contrast to the loneliness I sometimes felt during the holidays. I went over to her house, and we hung out and ate some food I had never tried before. It was honestly a really nice vibe, and I enjoyed it a lot.

That evening, neither of us really wanted the night to end, so she asked me if I knew how to play Spades. I told her that I did, so I called up some friends to see if they wanted to come over and play some Spades with us. The energy in the room was electric as we laughed and challenged each other to fierce competitions. They did, and we ended up having a ton of fun. A couple of days later, we went to the movies together and grabbed a bite to eat afterward.

Every moment felt effortless as if we were picking up right where we left off. We spent a lot of time just talking again about life, our hometowns, who we'd been hanging out with recently, and what type of people we were into. That's when I told her that I was bisexual. I told Star that I liked men and women and that I actually preferred to have them both at the same time and wasn't really into one-on-one relationships. She was surprised but said it was cool.

At this point, we would hang out on a weekly basis, especially during the weekends, to play Spades and just spend quality time together. The bond we were forming was intense, each shared a laugh and secret, weaving us closer together. We would hang out in her heated pool with friends and other couples I would invite over. It was always really nice, and we always seemed to have a good time together. Since things were going so well, we decided to make it official and started dating each other exclusively. There was an undeniable chemistry between us that felt different from anything I had experienced before.

Star started coming to my house and to my events (not as a participant but as a staff member), which was very advantageous for me because the truth is, Star was very beautiful. Her beauty was mesmerizing; she had this way of commanding attention without even trying. She would have different colored hair, eyes and really go all out with her makeup and her overall look. She was so exotic that everyone at my parties (both old and new members alike) wanted to know who she was. In fact, I used to have men come right up to me, asking what they had to do to get with her—and they were willing to do anything and everything for a moment with Star. Their eagerness was both flattering and amusing, a testament to her magnetic allure. They would even ask me if they could give me anything I wanted, just to have a moment of her time.

And to add to the ever-growing curiosity, she would always introduce herself as Mrs. Yolo. It was a playful twist that intrigued people even more, sparking conversations and raising eyebrows. It was so amusing to me how obsessed everyone was with Star, especially since no one thought I could get a woman of that caliber when, in fact, my whole life, I've only dated these types of women because that is all I am attracted to.

Plus, I would always laugh when people would come up to me during the party telling me, "Oh hey, we met your wife, Mrs. Yolo!" I would say, "My wife?! Nope, that's my girlfriend," but I still thought it was funny.

But in truth, it was easier for her to introduce herself as my wife so other men at the party would not attack or try to continue pursuing her because she was off-limits. It created a sense of protection around our relationship, a boundary that kept others at bay. They knew better than to go after the host's woman. It gave them just enough fear to know they could easily get banned from my events if they did something wrong or unwanted. In many ways, it solidified our bond, reinforcing the idea that we were a team navigating this social landscape together. Things were getting better and better for me.

Chapter 11 – Jacuzzi Night

One night, Star and I decided to invite a few friends over for cards and drinks, a familiar ritual for us. Nights like these usually revolved around spades games, where we'd team up, trash talk, and let competitive energy mix with laughter and lighthearted arguments. My partner was John, a quiet guy who had a surprisingly sharp mind for the game, while Star's partner was Jessica, who always brought an easygoing charm and a bold streak to the table. The atmosphere was filled with the sound of shuffling cards, clinking glasses, and bouts of laughter that rose and fell with each hand we played.

As the night wore on, winning and losing rounds, drinks flowed more freely, and so did the conversations. Slowly, the room filled with a charge, an unspoken connection growing with every look and laugh. Eventually, someone suggested that we move to the heated pool. We called it the "jacuzzi" because of the way the warmth and the steamy enclosure made it feel like a cozy, intimate spa, even though it was a full-sized pool.

Once in the water, the alcohol relaxed us all, allowing inhibitions to slip away. We started sharing stories about our lives, then, bit by bit, about our past relationships, our fantasies, and our curiosities. Jessica got a bit shy with the direction the conversation was taking and eventually excused herself, mentioning an early shift in the morning. That left Star, John, and me in the pool together, taking shots, sharing glances, and testing the boundaries of our comfort zones.

There was a moment when I caught John's eye and sensed his intrigue as he watched Star and me. Fueled by curiosity and the edge of the moment, I leaned in to kiss Star, letting John witness the closeness between us. His eyes darkened with a mix of curiosity and anticipation, and as Star leaned into the kiss, we could see John tension shift, the line between friend and something more starting to blur.

I suggested we play a game, "Do or Drink," which was our way of saying that everyone would either do a dare or take a shot. This was a game where secrets could be uncovered and desires tested. With each new card drawn, the challenges became bolder, pushing us closer to territories we hadn't dared to tread before. We pulled a card that read, "Three-way kiss." Star and I had done this kind of thing before, but for John, it was new, and he laughed nervously, asking, "Wait, all of us, like… at the same time?"

Star nodded, leaning in with a wicked grin. "All together."

As our lips met in a three-way kiss, there was a surprising intensity to it, a thrill that seemed to take us all off guard. Each of us tasted the unfamiliar sensation, the shared warmth, and the mingling breath. It was as if we were discovering each other in a new way, breaking down barriers that had once felt untouchable.

After that, something shifted within John. I could tell he was experiencing a side of himself he hadn't encountered before. Star and I exchanged a look, and I knew it was time to take things further. I turned to John with a playful challenge. "You're known for being the best at going down… why don't you show Star what you can do?"

He hesitated for a second, his eyes searching mine, and then he gave a small, tentative smile. "For real?"

"Yeah," I said, giving him a reassuring nod. "For real."

We made our way into the bedroom, the energy between us sizzling with anticipation. John began to explore this new experience with Star, and I watched the exchange, letting the excitement build within me. Soon, I found myself joining in, each of us merging in a rhythm that was exhilarating and foreign yet surprisingly natural. There were moments when my own boundaries felt tested, each new sensation adding a new layer to the experience.

As I moved between John and Star, we found ourselves lost in the pure thrill of letting go, each moment bringing a new depth to our connection. In one moment, Star was riding John Face as I was standing up behind; I thrust my dick into her super wet …. Slowly stroking, letting my dick come all the way out, hitting John on the lips. After a few times, John allowed it to enter his mouth. The sense of controlling and bringing a darker side out of someone gave me intense pleasure. I jizz in Star.

Afterward, as the intensity faded and we sat at the edge of the bed, John looked at me with a mix of wonder and uncertainty. He asked, "Does that make me… you know, am I gay now?"

I chuckled softly, resting a hand on his shoulder. "Man, it was just us, just a moment. It doesn't define you; it's just something we all share. A fantasy we explored together. Besides, you're still my spades partner. That's what really counts, right?"

He nodded, smiling a little as relief washed over him, knowing that the night was simply a chapter in our friendship—a twist we hadn't expected but one that had shown us all a different side of ourselves.

Chapter 12 – Houston

Fast forward to January – I invited Star to accompany me to a friend's birthday party. The theme of the party was upscale Roman Gods and Goddesses, so of course, out of the 120 people there, I was the only out-of-shape guy. True to the theme, everyone else was chiseled perfectly and, of course, with dicks down to their ankles.

The women were fairly fit and attractive. In other words, this was a party for the Elites. Despite all that, we hung out and took photos, put on a show for a couple of people, and turned a few people down who wanted to join in. After the party, we had a few people come to our hotel room where we were staying, and we all turned up together.

Star loved the fact that I was really only into mostly fucking her because not only were there no other women that I was really attracted to, but she was able to turn up with other guys because I also wanted to turn up with them, so it was a bonus for her.

The morning after, we headed to the airport to fly back to the sunshine state. In all honesty, it almost seemed too good to be true. And, of course, my intrusive thoughts were right…

I learned that she was in a relationship – she was actually married to a sailor in the U.S. Navy. She had told me she was also former U.S. Navy and was receiving full disability benefits ($10K per month, tax-free).

When I confronted her, she told me that her "friend" was just an opportunity so she could get a better house and have fewer bills to pay. But, she said that all of that had changed because she had met me and we had found this new relationship together so she had called it off.

I believed what she told me was true, so I had no reason to doubt her because I had actually heard her having conversations with the guy discussing their breakup and how their relationship was going to end. I didn't really feel worried and trusted her to keep her word.

One day, as usual, we were at her house playing Spades with some people. Her neighbor was out and about and saw us together. I didn't think anything of it, of course. But, unbeknownst to me, her neighbor was friends with one of the guys she was currently in a relationship with for over 9 years.

Of course, not knowing that we were together and assuming Star was hooking up with someone else, the neighbor did the right thing and called the guy to tell him I was there with her and how it looked like Star had gotten herself a new boyfriend. She went as far as describing me to him, saying I was a lot younger than she was since she was in her 40s and at the time I was in my 30s.

The guy ended up calling her to confront her, so we, of course, ended up having to have a conversation about it. Once again, she assured me that they were no longer together but that the only reason she still maintained communication with him was because he had taken money from her that he never paid back. So, she was hoping one day he would return that money and that was the reason why she still kept in contact with him. I was cool with that – life went on.

We kept going out regularly and even began to travel together. Life was so good that it was almost as if I had forgotten that less than a year ago, I had been in a totally different relationship with another couple. When we reached around the 6th or 7th month together, she felt that we should take the next step as a couple. She said, "you know, we should get married." I told Star that I did not want to get married to anyone else ever again. That isn't my thing – I am not looking for it. In fact, I will never propose to someone again.

Visibly disappointed, she dropped the topic and left it alone. But, shortly after, she brought it up again and said "well, then I will propose to you." I laughed it off and ignored her comment not thinking into it.

Randomly, Star told me she wanted to take me out to dinner, and she asked me where I would want to go eat. I told her that instead of dinner, since it was my choice, we should go out to The Grand Lux Café since I love their brunch menu. She said sure and told me to invite some of my friends. I invited most of my Lifestyle friends (which I honestly consider family because here in Florida, I do not have anyone).

At the restaurant, as we ordered our food, she interrupted everyone abruptly and told me she wanted to talk to me in front of everyone. She turned to me and explained that the last few months by my side have been great.

The way I've treated her, how I've opened her eyes to the Lifestyle, the way I've made her feel comfortable and safe, and the way she sees me doing well for myself as a successful man are all reasons why she wants to marry me. She popped the question in front of everyone and all I could do is laugh. In my mind, I was like "there is no way this chick is about to propose to me." I kept goofing off and sure enough, she pulled out a ring and proposed to me in front of everyone. I laughed and said yes.

I'll admit, I was very pessimistic about the entire thing because I felt things between us were moving way too fast. I know I am a challenging and difficult person, and I own that. I started staying at her house more often since we were officially engaged at this point. I would spend a lot more time with her daughter and we would go out of town together on a regular basis.

Sometime later, Star felt obligated to divulge some information to me regarding her ex. She warned me to please be careful and to watch my back because she thought that her ex was following me around and apparently he was a very dangerous person. She painted this picture of the guy for me to what I am guessing was an attempt to make me be aware of how dangerous he was – almost like she wanted me to be warned and borderline fearful of him. What Star didn't understand is that I am a Baltimore boy from the hood. So back home, if you knew someone was coming after you, the rule of the streets of Baltimore says to get them before they get you. I wasn't too worried, to be honest. I told her okay and kept about our lives.

One night, while she stayed at my house, my doorbell notified me that there was someone at my front door. Keep in mind it is 5 o'clock in the morning. I checked my camera with my phone, and lo and behold, it is one of her exes. I turned to her and asked her, "Hey, is this your ex?"

She said, "Yeah, oh my god…" Of course, I jumped out of bed and looked for clothes to throw on real quick. I put on some shorts and a t-shirt and ran down my stairs to catch him.

When I opened my front door, there was a car speeding off. I went back upstairs and told Star he was no longer there. After about an hour, she told me she was going to go get ready to head home because later on, she had a dentist appointment. I told her okay, and then she left for her house and took her usual morning walk.

When she left my house, I started thinking to myself about how I wanted to confront her ex for coming to my house like that. I called Star and asked her for his phone number, and she gave it to me without hesitation. I called the number, and he answered. I called him by name, Craig, and I asked, "Do you know who I am?" He said yes, but at the time, he was with his grandkids and could not talk. Craig asked if I could call him back in about 5 minutes. I obliged…

Chapter 13 – Craig

Once again, following the raw, unedited truth throughout this book, and in the spirit of continued transparency, I have not altered the following dialogue:

Craig: hello?

Me: yeah

Craig: yeah what's going on brother?

Me: nothing much…working away

Craig: okay ok. Yeah I just wanted to apologize to you brother. I didn't mean to disrespect your house. You know, sometimes people get in their little feelings

Me: mmhmmm

Craig: yeah so…I apologize

Me: ok

Craig: I hope you accept my apology. It won't happen again

Me: nah, I'm good. I just want to make sure everything else is ok. I'm like I don't know this guy like…I don't know

Craig: no I wasn't there to fight anybody or anything like that you know what I'm saying sooo…. you know I am the type of person who keep it 100%. Whatever you doing whatever you got going on just keep it 100%. You understand what I saying? I don't want anybody to be…you don't gotta lie to me that's all I ask – keep it 100%

Me: right

Craig: whatever you doing, this, that, and the third you know what I mean that's what I think. Keep it 100%

Me: right

Craig: she said there ain't nothing going on. What she say to me was that, ain't no man spending the night at a women house unless they fucking

Me: (chuckle)

Craig: I said the same thing – am I wrong now? Keep it 100%

Me: no, you are absolutely right but, are ya'll together?

Craig: are we together?

Me: uh huh?

Craig: uhhh yeah you can say that you can say that. I won't lie to you. I've been with Star for a lil' bit. We don't part ways whatever-whatever

Me: you said ya'll didn't part ways?

Craig: I said yeah we parted ways

Me: right!

Craig: we still friends or whatever-whatever

Me: mmhmmm. Right. I thought ya'll wasn't together but ya'll were together for a long time so…

Craig: right right…but she married now.

Me: right, and that's ending.

Craig: say again?

Me: and that's, ending

Craig: I don't know…I don't know until I see paperwork

Me: right

Craig: a lot of people say a lot of things but they don't happen

Me: right. I've seen it…so…

Craig: you seen it?

Me: mmhmm

Craig: she's the type of person that if she say something then she ain't got no problems showing it. She's that type of person

Me: mmhmm

Craig: she aint showed me…not that you know, she had to…you know what I'm saying?

Me: right…ok. I just wanted to know

Craig: I don't know…you know, people tell you things and then it doesn't pan out to what it be because like I said, even when she told me she was going to Dallas, Texas there, I was like well I was in

Houston, and she got mad with me with this, that, and the third when I told her all you had to do was keep it real.

Me: mmhmm

Craig: what's wrong with keeping it real? If that's who you with then that who you with. You ain't gotta say you went to one place and went to another.

Me: right

Craig: correct?

Me: no, I agree. Totally agree.

Craig: you ain't gotta lie. Keep it 100%

Me: that's right

Craig: you keep it 100%, people will respect you well.

Me: yup, they respect the truth

Craig: exactly. Give her the truth, give me the truth – no matter what it is. But like I said, you into, whatever you into, I ain't got no problem I'll do it with you.

Me: (chuckle)

Craig: I kept it 100%. Is that not 100%?

Me: yeah absolutely

Craig: and I told her, I ain't got a problem with it. if that's what you're into, I'll do it with you. But don't lie, that's what you want to do

Me: why do you think she lying? Or…

Craig: listen man…I've been dealing with her for a long time…how long have ya'l been friends?

Me: ahhhh…for about half a year?

Craig: so I've known her for over 8-years

Me: yeah I know, well I know that yeah

Craig: so, I know when somebody is telling me the truth and not telling the whole story

Me: uh huh

Craig: see this the first I ever heard of you…and, they always telling me they ain't got no friends and then I say well I don't you ever bring these friends around, then you say you ain't, you don't know who I hang with…I don't judge nobody on what they do or how they do…I don't have a problem with that. I am friends with anybody.

Me: uh huh

Craig: I don't judge people – I'm cool with you. Im sure about my sexuality…you understand what I am saying?

Me: uh huh

Craig: so, that's just me, you know…but if you tell me one thing and then it don't pan out to what it be I know how you are cause this the first I ever heard of you and I've been you know going out with her for 8-years and now all of a sudden ya'll best of friends…I understand. People meet people and you know get good vibes and ya'l become friends – you understand what I am saying?

Me: uh huh

Craig: and I understand it so…keep it real, keep it 10%. That's all I am saying. You into ménage à trois, I ain't got no problem doing it with you – let me be in on it.

Me: (chuckles)

Craig: why you laughing?

Me: I'm just laughing cause how you saying "let me get in on it" it's just funny to that's all

Craig: I' telling you the truth I'm saying let me get in on it

Me: so, my understanding ya'll was together and its over, and, yeah I know she married that guy and that's over with so…and we're dating, so, its like "oh ok," so all I know you as is the "ex" and I was like "oh well ok, he's the ex this is good." Then I was like "oh wait you reached out to me on Facebook what is this?" And then this morning I couldn't get fast enough – like, you were gone time I made it (Craig cuts me off)

Craig: I was out there, I was out there for about 5-10 minutes and then you know, I left ain't wanna make no scene. If that's what you saying then let it be know. Keep it 100%. You would've came outside and said this is this, this is this….she told me you gay. I don't know –

Me: yeah…interesting (chuckles)

Craig: well don't go back and tell her cause she'll get mad with me and all that but that's what she told me

Me: I don't care, that stuff don't phase me, ok? People called me many'o names and many'a things

Craig: so are ya'l dating or doing your thing?

Me: yup

Craig: ya'll dating?

Me: yes we are

Craig: see I asked her that she didn't tell me that

Me: hmm, I don't know when the last time you spoke with her but, hmmm yeah its been like that for a couple of months

Craig: well she didn't, she didn't tell me. I asked her to tell me the truth. I said "just tell me the truth that ya'll dating and I'm cool with that"

Me: uh huh

Craig: she said ya'll not dating ya'll friends. She told me you was gay.

Me: uh huh…no (chuckles)

Craig: well I'm glad you told me the truth but you know I respect that. But she didn't, well I don't want you or her to fall out

Me: oh no I am not gonna fall out, I am a different type of dude man that's why I called you. I am not, uh, yeah I don't, I am a different type of dude

Craig: oh ok cause…well, like today, like I apologized to her for this, that, and the third, and, uh, my bad bro all I ask from her was the truth bro. That's all I asked for was the truth. That's why you know – like I told, she said, uh…I don't want ya'll to fall out man

Me: oh we not gonna fall out. I promise you that.

Craig: but she lied to you, right?

Me: lied to me about what?

Craig: nah I don't wanna…

Me: no, I am asking you – lied to me about what? Because I knew about you…I knew that ya'll was together for a while but ya'll not in a relationship and you all haven't been in a relationship for a while – I know that you had your, you know your occasional sex hookups…you know for a little bit

Craig: right

Me: and that's it. I mean, there's nothing else there I guess…unless I am missing something?

Craig: no, no, no, no…but, you know you gave it to me raw and that's all I asked for was, the truth. So how long ya'll been having relationships if you don't mind me asking?

Me: it's been a couple of months.

Craig: couple months?

Me: yeah. She was probably still, you know, meeting you when we as together – maybe – I don't know but, you know that's not (Craig cuts me off)

Craig: I believe she was I believe she was

Me: if she's not in a committed relationship with you and wasn't in a committed relationship with me, you know, that doesn't even matter. That's stuff don't matter

Craig: that's true, that's true

Me: in only matters when (Craig cuts me off)

Craig: so ya'll in a committed relationship now?

Me: right

Craig: oh ok. I understand that brother. That wont happen again me coming to your house brother.

Me: and that's it. So, I was like "damn that was my opportunity to talk to him face to face shit I was like damn." I just knocked out so

Craig: I understand. Yeah Ima keep it real with you she might not call me no more whatever you know. She came here, went to lunch with me today and my homeboy birthday she came to Houston's…so I don't know what she told you.

Me: mmhmmm

Craig: so, like I told her Ima keep it 100% I told her why we both can't do

Me: (chuckles)

Craig: I kept it 100%. If that's what you like, I ain't got no problem me and you both doing it. I told her that. I don't know if you get down like that or whatever-whatever but I told her that4

Me: okay. And what did she say?

Craig: she just kept saying that she ain't messing with you. Ya'll just friends.

Me: okay

Craig: so I listen, you ain't gotta go back and say nothing I don't want no

Me: dude, I don't do the drama I don't do none of that stuff

Craig: so, so, can I ask you another question you keep it real? Since we talking?

Me: sure

Craig: so ya'll swinging?

Me: are we swinging? Ahh I wouldn't call it swinging per se

Craig: what you call it?

Me: oh you mean am I in the *Lifestyle*? I am definitely in the *Lifestyle*.

Craig: oh ok. So, you go both ways?

Me: I sure do

Craig: ok so, how she even got attached to you? That's what I am trying to figure out you go both ways

Me: this is not my first time being in a relationship with a woman I've been married twice…I've got grown kids

Craig: yeah, I understand that but I'm saying how ya'll even got it…so ya'll doing things together with other people?

Me: not really. We just chilling. We getting to know each other. Yeah we have friends that's in the *Lifestyle* and stuff like that but really we be just chilling and getting to know each other.

Craig: but I've been had told her you know I know she like to like to dab and if that's what you like then come on out – stop hiding

Me: so what happened?

Craig: I don't know for some reason she doesn't want to do that with me. I don't know if she didn't want me to see her in that type of lifestyle but I've been do that and I said I didn't have no problem and that I would do it with her.

Me: mmhmmm

Craig: it doesn't get no realer than that brother. But for some reason, I don't I know I guess she felt…I don't know I am assuming she think I may look down on her whatever. So I am telling you, I will do it with you so what's the problem?

Me: right

Craig: then I told her then why don't I come over there with you? Oh they tight people this, that, and the third da-da-da

Me: okay

Craig: I ain't gonna lie to you

Me: that's good. I mean, I knew it was something like "this dude not poppin' up off of nothing. There's gotta be still feeling or something like that."

Craig: yeah. See, she ain't keeping it real with you then cause, Im going to give you a prime example: she came home one day this, that, and the third, we bout' to have sex, I touched the pussy and it was oozing out with cum so I said "you must of went with buddy." She said "no I wasn't, I swear, I swear to you." I am a man I know, I know. I'm not stupid.

Me: mhmmm

Craig: you not stupid right?

Me: nope not at all

Craig: oh ok, so…then she was like "oh, we not doing nothing da-da-da…" keep it real – that's all I ask. Keep it real. I can tell you uhhhh, she came home, I think she probably just left your house – she came home, she was ready to go walking or whatever and we went and got coffee, this, that, and the third and then we went in the house this and that…I still, even though that still happened I still, you know, I still fucked her

Me: mmhmmm (chuckles)

Craig: why you laughing?

Me: no I'm listening to the story

Craig: so I told her, why me and you can't do it? I can watch you fuck him.

Me: mmhmmm

Craig: I don't have a problem with it. You have a problem with it?

Me: I don't care

Craig: well can I watch?

Me: chuckles…ahh I think you are ahh, in a certain category right now

Craig: what's the category I am in?

Me: I don't know I think ya'll need to mend whatever relationship or whatever issue that ya'll have going on hmmm, yeah, I don't know its something going on between ya'll two. And I don't know what it is. And I know, 9-years is a lot to give up I don't know who gave it up or which one of ya'll gave it up or whatever the case may be but, it is my understanding that she moved on a little bit and you moved on a little bit – both of ya'll have ya'll own situations going on and that's just it. So, I don't know something is missing there

Craig: yeah well you know, I ain't gonna lie we still care for each other but like I said, if I am willing to be in that type of lifestyle, the things you doing why I can't participate?

Me: mmhmmm. So ya'll never do that?

Craig: she act like she don't wanna do it. I don't know why. That's what I am saying – let me come over there and watch. I ain't got a problem with it. Do you?

Me: nope, I don't care. I am not that guy. I told you, I am a different type of dude.

Craig: so, I ain't got a problem with it. Can you explain that to her?

Me: I sure will

Craig: I want to watch – I want to see her get pounded.

Me: what else would you like to see?

Craig: I want to see her – I want to see what's going on

Me: you want to see what's going on (chuckles) – that ain't telling me nothing (chuckles)

Craig: I want to see what's going on bro. I want to see ya'll freaking. Ya'll freaking I want to watch I ain't got not problem with it. I'll participate

Me: he said "I'll participate," alright (chuckles)

Craig: God-dam right. I'll participate. I ain't fucking scared I ain't ever been scared.

Me: alright

Craig: you know

Me: you'll what?

Craig: hey listen I don't know if you got somebody else on the phone

Me: dude there ain't anybody else on the phone. You got Facetime? I can call you (chuckles) live

Craig: call me ummm, I'm on Facebook

Me: no, Facetime – I'm talking about Facetime

Craig: oh, I don't have an iPhone

Me: oh ok

Craig: listen brother, I don't have a problem. If ya'll fucking tonight, I can come over there. I wanna watch. Hey, I'm dead serious I wanna watch. Can I come through?

Me: I will talk to her and see what she says

Craig: I want to come through, I want to watch, let me participate.

Me: participate how?

Craig: since you fucking her, I wanna eat the pussy

Me: while I am doing that?

Craig: God-damn right – I ain't scared

Me: (chuckles)

Craig: why you laughing?

Me: cause, that shit hot. Nigga, I'm laughing cause that shit is hot. So I'm laughing, like (Craig cuts me off)

Craig: I'm into that shit bro I kept telling her that. She the one that don't, like she don't believe me, she don't I don't know. I can't explain why she wont bro. I been trying – listen, I swear on everything bro I've been trying to get her to do this. She kept saying she don't know no body she don't know nobody

Me: mmhmmm

Craig: I told her I'd do it I ain't got no problem with it.

Me: what all are you into?

Craig: man…you'll see. Let me come on over.

Me: nah I need to know so I know

Craig: listen man, oh, I'm not into no dude fucking me in the ass, no I ain't into that. I ain't into that brother

Me: right (chuckles)

Craig: that's what you trying to ask me?

Me: no, I'm asking what all you are into that's what I asking you

Craig: nah I am not into getting fucked in the ass – I am not into fucking a man in the ass

Me: mmhmm

Craig: nah-nah…now if you wanna freak her I'll do it with you.

Me: mmhmmm (chuckles)

Craig: what that's what you into getting fucked in the ass?

Me: nope I didn't say that. I am asking what all are you into. Ok? That's what I said

Craig: okay. Just like, when I came ya'll probably was already over there participating.

Me: and when is this?

Craig: this morning

Me: this morning negro I was knocked out

Craig: oh you was knocked out? Oh okay…so, you and her, ya'll did anal?

Me: what did you say?

Craig: you and her, ya'll did anal?

Me: yeah

Craig: I've been trying to get her to do that with me for the longest but she won't do it

Me: hmm that's why I said I said, I don't know it's hard to believe that ya'll haven't done stuff like that…but

Craig: man, we've done anal but she's was like "ohhh that hurt" and she ain't wanna do it maybe you as smooth talker I don't know

Me: he said a "smooth talker" nahh I ain't a smooth talker I'm just real buddy, honest (Craig cuts me off)

Craig: no I'm just saying you probably smooth talked her into doing it but, I don't know why she won't do it with me brother I can't explain it but I tried to do all that with her bro

Me: mmm okay

Craig: I tried, so

Me: do you have a lady?

Craig: huh?

Me: I said, do you have a lady now?

Craig: nah

Me: oh okay. So you still single.

Craig: yeah

Me: okay – that's whats up

Craig: let me ask you, are ya'll having unprotected sex? Since ya'll wasn't doing this, that and the third. Ya'll probably having unprotected sex correct?

Me: (chuckles)

Craig: why you laughing?

Me: dude cause you asking a lot of specific questions

Craig: cause you know, people lie to you bro and then don't keep it real all I ask is to keep it real. You say you keep it real so keep it real

Me: absolutely – absolutely

Craig: so what's the answer?

Me: absolutely

Craig: so that's the answer? Ya'll having unprotected sex?

Me: if that's what you call it

Craig: okay. See that's what I'm saying that's all I'm asking – keep it real. What's so hard about that? I'm surprised she gave you my number how did you get my number?

Me: I asked for it. I told you, I am a different type of dude. I don't know, how you know me, or where you know me from, or who told you about me, or whatever the case may be – I am a different type of dude I'm not these south Florida niggas at all

Craig: yeah I can tell you different cause any other one would've been like this and that – this and that – I can tell I respect that. And that's all I asked her man, keep it real, keep it 100%. That's all you can ask for, right?

Me: so yeah

Craig: you keep it 100% people respect you and that's all I ever asked her, keep it 100%

Me: yup

Craig: but…let me watch the show. Can I watch the show?

Me: I'll ask her

Craig: you ain't got a problem with it right?

Me: nope

Craig: ok well ask her

Me: oh I am going to ask her

Craig: yeah I will come through tonight. I was gonna go back home but I'll wait cause I wanna come through

Me: (chuckles) he said "I'll wait"

Craig: yeah I am. I wanna come through

Me: I will ask her and see what she says

Craig: you didn't have to block your number – we grown men bro

Me: that's right I just…dude – you gotta understand, I blocked my number because I am like "I'm calling this guy" it's because of your behaviors of why I blocked my number

Craig: but we straight bro – you can call me from your number

Me: ok? And that's why

Craig: okay. But we straight, you can call my number. Hey, let me come through and participate. I ain't gotta problem with it – you ain't gotta a problem with it so. Can you call me through your number that way we got numbers?

Me: yeah I sure will

Craig: and whatever my business is your business nobody elses – you understand?

Me: yeah

Craig: alright, so call me back with your number brother

Me: alright

Craig: alright thank you

Me: you're welcome

Chapter 14 – The Last Question

Immediately after getting off the phone with Craig, I said to myself, "Yup…let me go talk to this girl." I got dressed and jumped in my car to confront Star. Once I arrived at her residential community, I entered the gate code to get in because I wanted to surprise her instead of calling her ahead as usual. I knocked on her door, and she invited me in.

As soon as I walked in, I said, "Hey, let's play the question game." Judging by her reaction, she already knew something was up. She replied, "Boy, what do you want? Just ask me the question." As soon as that last word left her lips, her front doorbell rang. Star went to the door to see who was there. Lo and behold, it was Craig.

Unbeknownst to me, Craig had seen me pull up to Star's house outside and decided to introduce himself to me. Star called me to come to the front because her ex was at the door. I told her to let him in, and I walked over to the door and sat on a massage table that Star had in the living room. Star went to a corner and just stood there as Craig greeted both of us. He looked toward me and said, "Hey! My new best friend."

Star looked at me, and I said, "Yeah, I talked to him on the phone."

Craig instantly turned towards Star and said, "Why him? Why do all these things with him and not me? I told you I will do whatever it takes to be with you. I just don't understand – why him?"

The whole time, Star is looking at him with a puzzled expression. I kept looking over at Star to see how she would respond to all this.

At this point, I made the decision in my mind that this would be the last day I would see this girl.

Star's silence spoke volumes, but her eyes gave away more than I expected. She looked torn, conflicted. Was this about love? Or about something deeper, a fear she had been hiding for too long? I couldn't tell. All I knew was I had seen enough to understand that I wasn't going to be anyone's second choice.

For a while, I sat there watching and listening as Craig continued to confront and ask Star questions. He told her some of the things we had discussed over the phone earlier to try and understand why she was doing all this. He even mentioned that he really wanted to have a threesome with us and everything he was willing to do to keep her.

The air in the room felt thick, as if every word spoken made it harder for any of us to breathe. Star wasn't saying much, and I could tell the pressure was building on her. I watched her eyes dart back and forth between Craig and me, trying to gauge my reaction, looking for something—approval? An escape?

Finally, Craig asked us if he could come over later that evening if we were fucking. I told Craig to ask her, but in my mind, I knew I wouldn't be there for that. I had no intention of sitting through that nonsense. The whole thing felt like a game, and I was tired of being a pawn. The truth was, I didn't want to be in the middle of their mess anymore.

After Craig left, I told Star I was leaving, too. I told her to enjoy her life as I got in my car and left. As I pulled out of her driveway, I felt a weight lift off my chest. It was a strange mix of relief and bitterness. I knew I had made the right choice to walk away, but part of me couldn't help but wonder what might have been if things had turned out differently.

The drive home felt like a blur, and I couldn't help but replay the entire encounter in my head. Was I too quick to judge? Could I have approached this whole situation differently? But the more I thought about it, the clearer it became—I had tried too hard, and I deserved more than what I was getting. The late-night phone calls, the ambiguous texts, the promises that never followed through. It wasn't fair to me.

Later that night, I couldn't shake the feeling that Star had been caught in a cycle she couldn't break, and I was just another part of it. A part of me wanted to reach out again, maybe give her one last chance, but another part, the stronger part, knew that walking away was the only way to truly free myself.

The hardest part of the whole ordeal wasn't leaving her behind but accepting that I wasn't going to have the closure I needed. It was just going to fade away, like a chapter in a book that gets skimmed over and forgotten. But I wasn't going to let that chapter define me.

And so, as I lay in bed later that night, staring up at the ceiling, I realized something: the love I was looking for wasn't going to come from someone who couldn't even choose herself. It had to come from me first. It was time for me to choose myself, to stop chasing after things that weren't meant to be. It was time to move forward, no matter how much it hurt.

A Letter to My Supporters

First and foremost, I want to express my deepest gratitude to Samuel Duperval, my incredible graphic designer. I know working with me hasn't always been easy, but your talent and dedication have been invaluable. To Eric Ocasio, thank you for your support as my scribe. Entering and navigating this new world with me must have been a wild ride, but your steady determination—perhaps the Marine in you—has helped bring our first project to completion.

I also want to take a moment to thank the powers that be for allowing me to publish this book—at least the first one—while my great-grandmother is still with us. It is my deepest hope, through grace, that she will one day have the chance to see my autobiography.

*To all my supporters, I'm thrilled to share that this is just the beginning. This is the first of six books I have in the works. Among them is my raw and unfiltered autobiography, *BmoreBorn!*, and another intriguing title, *KEISHA*. These stories are deeply personal, and I'm so grateful to have the opportunity to share them with you.*

My hope is that through these books, I can open minds and touch hearts, reminding us all that life is unpredictable yet worth living to the fullest. While the characters' names have been changed to protect identities, the stories themselves remain true.

Thank you once again for being part of this journey with me. Your support means the world, and I can't wait to share more of my world with you.

With gratitude,

Shawn Dwayne Davis, Jr

YOLO

About the Author

Shawn Dwayne Davis Jr. is a trailblazer in every sense of the word. As the firstborn of many (8-15) siblings, Shawn found himself breaking barriers and setting examples throughout his life. Born and raised in the streets of Baltimore City, Maryland, to a drug kingpin parent, Shawn faced extraordinary challenges early on. Recognizing that his circumstances were far from ordinary, he sought a way out. With the help of his great-grandmother and law enforcement, he was removed from a chaotic environment and placed into a nurturing home where his life took a transformative turn.

In this new chapter, Shawn thrived. He became deeply involved in the church, directing the choir, leading the youth department, and even becoming an ordained minister. While excelling in his spiritual journey, he also broke new ground as a founding member of his high school's Gay-Straight Alliance, boldly coming out as a bisexual teen in the Baltimore City Paper. This decision ultimately cost him his place in the church but strengthened his resolve to create his own path.

Driven by an entrepreneurial spirit, Shawn discovered a passion for hard work, holding over 40 jobs in his first 30 years before finding long-term success at Wells Fargo holding many postions such credit manager, store manager and a VP just to name a few . However, recognizing the limitations placed on him because of his identity, he took the leap to start his own businesses, Placid Lifestyle , Yolo Ent., and Yolo Consulting. These ventures—once hidden due to societal expectations—have become thriving enterprises, including a successful condom distribution business.

Beyond his professional achievements, Shawn is a global traveler, a culinary enthusiast, and an active member of organizations like The Black Naturist Association, Chi Sigma Delta Fraternity Inc., and Habitat for Humanity.

With a life motto of You Only Live Once (YOLO), Shawn continues to inspire others to embrace their truth, overcome challenges, and live life to its fullest potential.